The Adventure Continues . . .

Hi! I'm Jackie. I love adventure. That's why I'm an archaeologist. My job is to search the world for ancient treasures. I study them to learn how people lived in the past.

My big adventure began when I found an eight-sided stone with a picture of a rooster on it. It turned out to be one of twelve magic talismans that are scattered across the globe.

But an evil group called The Dark Hand is looking for the talismans. If they find all twelve, they will have the power to rule the Earth!

It's up to me to protect the world from their evil plan. I already have some of the talismans. And I know where the rat talisman is, too.

But you'd never believe where it ends up!

A PARACHUTE PRESS BOOK

TM and © 2002 Adelaide Productions, Inc. All Rights Reserved.

Published by Grosset & Dunlap, a division of Penguin Putnam Books for Young Readers, New York. GROSSET & DUNLAP is a trademark of Penguin Putnam, Inc. Published simultaneously in Canada. Printed in U.S.A.

Library of Congress Cataloging-in-Publication Data is available.

ISBN 0-448-42671-4
A B C D E F G H I J

JACKIE CHAN
ADVENTURES™ #8

The Power of the Rat

A novelization by Megan Stine
based on the teleplay "Tough Break"
written by David Slack

Grosset & Dunlap

Chapter 1

"That's the ugliest lamp I've ever seen," the woman beside Jackie Chan said. She squirmed in her seat in the crowded auction room. "It even has a rat painted on it. How tacky."

"A rat?" Jackie asked, perking up. Could it be the talisman he had been waiting for?

He followed the woman's gaze. She was looking at the auctioneer at the front of the room.

The man held up a lamp, ready to sell it to the highest bidder.

Jackie spotted an eight-sided stone set in the base of the lamp. A picture of a black rat was painted in the center of the stone.

It *is* a talisman! Jackie thought.

It was one of the twelve ancient Chinese charms that had been scattered across the globe. All of the talismans were magical. They brought amazing power to whoever possessed them.

An evil group called The Dark Hand wanted the talismans. If they captured all twelve, they would gain the power to rule the world!

That was why Jackie agreed to help Section Thirteen find the talismans first. Section Thirteen was a top-secret U.S. government agency.

"Do I hear a bid for this lamp with the rat design?" the auctioneer asked.

"One hundred dollars!" Jackie cried.

"Wonderful," the auctioneer said. "Do I hear one hundred and fifty?"

"Two hundred dollars," a deep voice boomed from the back of the room.

Jackie whirled around to see who was bidding against him. His heart sank. It was Tohru, the enormous enforcer who worked for Valmont— the leader of The Dark Hand.

"Two hundred fifty!" Jackie called out, raising his bid.

"Fantastic," the auctioneer said. "Do I hear—"

"Three hundred!" Tohru shouted.

"Three fifty!" Jackie replied.

"Four hundred!" Tohru shouted.

The bidding went on until Tohru bid one thousand dollars!

"Two thousand!" Jackie cried out in a panic. That was all the money he had left. I hope Tohru doesn't bid any higher, he thought.

Tohru turned to the two other enforcers with him—Finn and Ratso. "More money," he said.

Finn and Ratso emptied their pockets. A few coins fell out, along with a pile of weapons.

"Sorry," Ratso said.

"I have two thousand dollars," the auctioneer said. "Going once . . . going twice . . ."

Hurry up! Jackie thought. His heart was pounding. He glanced over

4

his shoulder and saw Tohru stomping down the aisle, toward the stage. Tohru was so large his head brushed the ceiling as he walked.

"Sold!" the auctioneer cried. "To Jackie Chan for two thousand dollars!"

But Tohru clearly didn't care about that. With one meaty fist, he knocked the auctioneer out of the way. Then he grabbed the lamp!

"Oh, no you don't!" Jackie leaped up. He ran across the tops of the chairs toward Tohru. Then he flew into a powerful spinning kick and knocked the lamp out of Tohru's hands.

Crash! The lamp shattered on the floor. The talisman broke free.

Jackie grabbed the talisman and

ran out of the auction room. "I'm-sorry-I'll-send-you-a-check-later!" he called to the auctioneer.

Outside the building, Jackie ran through a dark alley. Tohru, Ratso, and Finn followed close behind him.

But something even worse was in *front* of Jackie—four Shadowkhan warriors, sent by The Dark Hand! The ninjas quickly flickered down the alley walls.

How do they *do* that? Jackie wondered. But there was no time to find out! He jumped over a high fence at the end of the alley.

The Shadowkhan quickly followed Jackie. They surrounded him, swinging long wooden poles.

Get me out of here! Jackie thought.

6

He dashed onto a small bridge.

He did not notice the sign nearby: DANGER. BRIDGE CLOSED, STAY AWAY.

The bridge was old and unstable. It was ready to be destroyed. Bundles of dynamite were tied to its beams.

"I have you now!" Tohru yelled from the end of the bridge.

Jackie glanced back just in time to see Tohru's look of glee. Tohru had spotted the handle that would blow up the dynamite.

"Bye, bye, Chan!" Tohru called. He pushed the handle.

Ka-boom!

Chapter 2

Jackie's eyes opened wide in horror. The bridge was exploding around him!

Dust and wood flew into the air. Pieces of metal broke apart. Two big pillars collapsed. The road beneath him started to fall away.

Jackie ran as the bridge crumpled under him. Panting, he raced up the crumbling roadway. Using it like a ramp, he leaped across to safety.

Ka-boom! Another explosion! The

whole bridge fell into a heap below.

"Where's the talisman?" Finn asked, watching from the far side of the bridge.

"It's buried . . . with Chan," Tohru replied.

That's what *they* think! Jackie thought with a smile. He slipped away into the night with the talisman safe in his pocket.

By the time Jackie returned home, his heart had stopped pounding so hard. But he was tired and dirty.

Jackie lived with his eleven-year-old niece, Jade. Their San Francisco apartment was inside the supersecret Section Thirteen headquarters.

"Hello, Jade," Jackie said to his niece. Then he noticed the living-room floor. It was covered with Jade's toys. "Wow! What a mess!"

Jade glanced up from her video game and laughed. Jackie was covered with dust. "Me?" she cried. "*You're* the mess, Jackie."

Maybe so, he thought. But at least I have the rat talisman!

Jackie stepped across a whole pile of toys. "Do baboons live here?" he asked. "Jade, you must learn to clean up after yourself."

"You got it, Jackie," Jade agreed. She jumped up and began to put away her things. "Hey, tell you what. I'll clean up the *whole place*—and you can give me a reward."

"What *kind* of reward?" Jackie asked.

"Oh, I don't know. . . ." Jade pretended to think about it. "How about a TurboTroll?"

"But you already have one of those." Jackie pointed to a big doll on the floor. It had spiky green hair and a shiny belt with an emerald jewel in its buckle.

"No way!" Jade said. "I only have a GnomeKop! TurboTroll is his mortal enemy. If I get both of them, they can fight each other! Can I have one? Please-please-please?"

"I'll think about it," Jackie replied, "*after* you've finished cleaning."

Jackie turned to leave. His foot landed right on Jade's GnomeKop.

"Whoaaaa!" Jackie cried as his legs slid out from under him. He flew into the air and somersaulted. He landed on the floor with a loud cracking crunch.

"Gnome power!" the toy shouted. Jackie's foot had hit the On switch. "Must find TurboTroll! Must find TurboTroll!"

Jade rushed to see if her toy was all right. She bent down and pressed a button on its back. The jewel in GnomeKop's belt glowed green.

"Belt blaster!" GnomeKop said.

"Phew!" Jade said. "Don't worry, Jackie. It's okay. Nothing's broken."

"Nothing's broken? That's what *you* think!" Jackie moaned from his spot on the floor. He winced in pain. "I think I broke my leg!"

Chapter 3

"It's all my fault," Jade mumbled as she sat beside Jackie the next day. She felt awful. Jackie's leg was in a cast. He couldn't walk, so he had to sit in a wheelchair.

"Run over an exploding bridge? No problem," Jackie's uncle said. "But step on a child's toy? You break your bones!" Uncle started laughing.

"I'm so sorry," Jade said for about the millionth time.

13

"It's okay, Jade," Jackie replied. "Accidents happen. But now do you see why it is important to clean up your toys?"

"Totally," Jade said. "I promise I'll keep them picked up." She tossed all her toys into the toy chest. She threw the GnomeKop on top.

"Must find TurboTroll!" the doll shouted. "Must find TurboTroll!"

"Jade," Jackie said, frowning at the toy. "Please turn that thing off."

"Sorry!" Jade reached into the toy chest as fast as she could. She removed the batteries from GnomeKop.

"Don't worry," Uncle said. "Jackie is young and strong. He will heal quickly. In the meantime," Uncle went on, "he can do research." He pushed Jackie's wheelchair toward a pile of books on a desk. Then he poured Jackie some hot tea. "Get started," he said, and he left the room.

Jade watched as Jackie searched through the books. He pulled the rat talisman out of his pocket and placed it on the desk.

Jade wished that she could help him. "Can I get you something?" she asked. "More tea, maybe?"

"No thanks, Jade," Jackie said without looking up.

Jade watched him for a few minutes.

"The power of the rat brings motion to the motionless," Jackie mumbled softly. "Hmm . . ."

"Need anything now?" Jade asked.

Jackie turned to Jade. "I need quiet so I can concentrate. Okay?" He started reading again.

"I'll just fluff your pillow," Jade said. She grabbed the pillow that was under Jackie's leg.

"Ow!" Jackie cried as his leg hit the floor. "Jade, maybe I should take care of myself," he said. "Remember, within every weakness lies strength."

"Whatever you say, Jackie," Jade replied. "But let me move you a little closer to the desk, so you can—"

"No! Don't!" Jackie cried as she pushed his wheelchair. His cast smacked into the desk. "Owwwww!"

"Sorry!" Jade hurried to tend to his leg. In her rush, she bumped his cup of steaming hot tea. It spilled onto his lap.

16

"Ow-ow-ow! Hot!" Jackie yelled. He jerked his leg and accidentally knocked the rat talisman off the desk.

"Sorry!" Jade cried. "Let's get some towels!" She ran behind the wheelchair, and steered Jackie out of the room.

They did not see the rat talisman fly into Jade's toy chest. It landed right inside GnomeKop's battery compartment.

Instantly, the toy sprang to life!

"Gnome power!" GnomeKop jumped up and climbed out of the toy chest—all by himself!

He sniffed the air, searching for trolls. "You cannot hide forever, Turbo-Troll!" GnomeKop grumbled.

Then he marched to the front door

of the apartment. "Belt blaster!" he cried.

In a flash, the green jewel in his belt buckle lit up. A powerful beam of light shot out. It melted the door-knob.

A moment later, GnomeKop kicked open the door and marched outside.

GnomeKop was alive—and he had escaped!

Chapter 4

"Where is the rat talisman?" Jackie asked as Jade wheeled him back to his desk.

Jade's gaze darted quickly around the room. Nothing else seemed to be missing. But the doorknob was melted.

"It's gone!" Jade cried. "Someone came in and stole it!"

"We must tell Captain Black," Jackie said, wheeling toward the door. Captain Augustus Black was Jackie's good friend, and the head of Section Thirteen.

Suddenly, a voice sounded over the speakers in the building. "Full alert! We have an intruder! Full alert!"

"He already knows." Jackie sighed with relief.

"I bet it's one of Valmont's guys," Jade said. "I don't know how he found this place, but I'll stop him before he can get away with the talisman!"

"No, Jade! Wait!" Jackie called. But in his wheelchair, he couldn't keep up with her.

Jade rushed out of the apartment and through the big government building. This is all my fault, she thought. If I hadn't spilled that tea, the rat talisman wouldn't be missing!

Jade dashed around a corner and spotted her GnomeKop marching down the hall.

"Must find TurboTroll," the doll said.

She skidded to a stop. Didn't she leave GnomeKop inside her toy chest? And didn't she take out his batteries? How did he get out here?

"Come here, you." She reached out to pick him up.

"Gnome power!" GnomeKop leaped into the air. He bounced off Jade's head and ran away.

Jade hurried back to tell Jackie what was happening. "Something's wrong with GnomeKop," she said really fast. "He's—"

"Please." Jackie held up his hands.

"I think I've heard all I want to hear about GnomeKop for one day."

"But, Jackie . . ." Jade began. Then she spotted GnomeKop sliding down a pipe behind Jackie. He leaped through the air—and landed on Jackie's face! "Look out!" Jade cried.

"Gnome power!" the toy shouted, and it attacked Jackie.

"Ahhh!" Jackie spun in his wheelchair, trying to get away from the toy. Finally, with one powerful tug, he plucked GnomeKop off and tossed him against a wall.

GnomeKop lay still for a moment. Then he stood up and darted away.

"That toy should be taken out of the stores," Jackie said. "It's dangerous!"

"That's what I was trying to tell

you," Jade explained. "He's not just a toy anymore. He's alive. *Alive!*"

"Motion to the motionless." Jackie gasped.

"Weird talisman power, huh?" Jade said.

Jackie nodded. "And we don't want Valmont to get his hands on *that* one, for sure!"

Meanwhile, back at The Dark Hand headquarters, Valmont was thinking just the opposite.

Deep inside his secret hideaway, he stood before the great and powerful Shendu. Shendu was an evil spirit trapped inside the statue of a dragon. He was the real leader of The Dark Hand.

"You must find the rat talisman," Shendu ordered Valmont. "It is the key to my freedom. It will turn me back into flesh and blood!"

Ratso, Finn, and Tohru stood shaking nearby.

"If you get the rat, will you get back all your dragon powers, too?" Ratso asked.

"No," Valmont replied. "Shendu must still have *all* the talismans for that."

Shendu's eyes glowed an angry shade of red. "Judging from experience, I will remain in this statue forever. And *you* will never lay eyes on the Lost Treasure!"

The treasure. That was the whole reason Valmont was working for Shendu. He had to have it.

Valmont turned to the three enforcers. "Bring me that talisman," he said. "And I don't care what you do to Jackie Chan to get it!"

". . . and the talisman must have dropped into the space for the battery and turned the toy into a living thing," Jackie was explaining to Captain Black.

Why does he even bother? Jade wondered. Captain Black doesn't believe in the magic of the talismans.

"Jackie, when you fell, did you hit your head?" Black asked.

Just then, something caught Jade's eye. GnomeKop was climbing up the wall behind Captain Black.

"Captain Black, GnomeKop is right

25

behind you!" Jade cried. "Look!"

The toy slipped into an air duct just as Captain Black turned his head.

"Jade, stop playing games," Black said.

"But he *was* behind you," Jackie said. "I saw him, too."

"Of course you did, Jackie." Black said. "Look, I've got to go. We'll talk about this later, okay?" He walked away, scratching his bald head.

"Come on, Jade," Jackie called. He wheeled himself toward the exit. "GnomeKop is on his way outside. We've got to catch him before he gets away."

Section Thirteen was underground. To leave, Jackie and Jade had to ride a secret elevator. It took them up into a phone booth on a quiet side street.

Once out of the booth, Jackie gazed around. He searched the streets for GnomeKop. "There he is!" he cried, pointing to a dead-end alley. He began to wheel toward the toy.

Jade jumped in front of him. "No, you have a broken leg," she said. "And GnomeKop is *my* responsibility."

Jade raced down the alley and quickly caught up with GnomeKop. This was her chance to prove that she could fix this mess. She bent down to pick him up. "Gotcha!"

In a flash, GnomeKop's emerald buckle lit up. "Belt blaster!" he shouted.

Zzzaaappp! A green bolt of energy shot out from the belt.

"Ahhh!" Jade gasped, jumping

away in surprise. She dropped the toy to the ground.

GnomeKop leaped up and quickly ran away.

"Stop him!" Jade called to Jackie, who was parked at the end of the alley.

As GnomeKop tried to escape, Jackie wheeled in front of him. But GnomeKop ran behind Jackie's chair, and gave it a push. "Gnome power!"

The chair began to roll down a steep hill. Slowly at first. Then faster . . . and faster!

"Whoaaaa!" Jackie cried, gripping the arms of his chair. I can't stop! he realized as he gained speed. I'm going to crash!

THE RAT TALISMAN

CARD 8

JACKIE CHAN
ADVENTURES ™

Tear at the dotted line to remove your card.

Hey, kids!
Check out this cool Jackie Chan Adventures trading card. There's one in each book. Collect them all!

The hunt for the rat talisman helps Jade discover her greatest strength!

FOUND: San Francisco, California.

WHERE: Set in the base of an old lamp.

POWER: Brings motion to the motionless!

The rat is one of the twelve signs of the Chinese zodiac. Want to know if *you're* a rat?

Look to see if you were born in any of the years below. Then check if your friends and family are rats, too!

Rat: 1948, 1960, 1972, 1984, 1996

RAT PERSONALITY

If you were born under the sign of the rat, you have a really *awesome* imagination. You also love movies. You always give everything your best shot—no matter what. And you expect others to do the same.

You'd make a really cool movie critic when you grow up!

Chapter 5

"The brakes!" Jackie cried. "Where are the brakes?" He zoomed down the steep hill.

Up ahead, some moving men were hauling a large table across the street.

"Look out!" Jackie warned them. Finally he found the brake handle and yanked on it as hard as he could.

"Aaaaahhhhhh!" Jackie yelled as the brake handle came off in his hands. The chair zoomed even faster!

The moving men quickly dropped the table in the street. Then they ran like crazy to get out of the way.

Two of the table's legs broke when they dropped it, leaving it propped up like a ramp.

"Whoaaaaaaa!" Jackie's wheelchair hit the ramp at high speed, and he flew into the air. The wheelchair fell away from him, but Jackie kept going. He sailed straight toward a banner hanging over the road.

The banner caught him!

"Huh?" Jackie's mouth dropped open. He couldn't believe his eyes. The banner he clung to was an ad for GnomeKops!

Jackie hung high above the street, gripping the banner. But then . . .

Riiipppppp!

I'm too heavy! he realized. His weight was tearing the banner. He was going to fall!

Below him, the two moving men were in the street again. This time they were pushing a sofa.

Jade ran up to the moving men and bumped them out of the way.

She grabbed the rolling sofa and shoved it under the banner. "Sorry— I'll-bring-it-right-back-thank-you!" Jade called to the movers.

The sofa rolled under Jackie just in time. Jackie landed in the soft cushions safely. "Oomph!"

Jade winced. "You didn't get hurt more, did you?" she asked.

Jackie didn't have time to answer.

Just then, he spotted GnomeKop.

"Where is TurboTroll?" GnomeKop said. Then the toy stopped in front of a billboard across the street. It was an ad for TurboTroll! A red arrow pointed toward Hayden Place Mall.

"Ah-ha!" GnomeKop shouted. "I will have TurboTroll's head!"

"Jade, we must follow him," Jackie said. "If GnomeKop finds TurboTroll at the mall, he'll use his belt blaster. Innocent people could be hurt."

"Right," Jade agreed. She pushed Jackie's wheelchair up the hill to the mall. This time she'd catch Gnome-Kop. This time she'd get it right.

They hurried into the mall's huge toy store. "Where did he go?" Jackie asked, looking everywhere.

"I know!" Jade whispered. She zoomed them straight to the action-figure aisle. There, Jade spotted GnomeKop, staring at a whole shelf filled with TurboTrolls.

"It is an army," GnomeKop said. "Gnome power!" He shot his belt blaster at the trolls. *Zzzaaappp! Zap!*

Screams rang throughout the store. People raced toward the exit.

As soon as GnomeKop stopped firing, Jade lunged at the toy.

But GnomeKop was too fast. He jumped away and ran to the next aisle. He hopped onto a shelf filled with hundreds of other GnomeKops. "Hide me, brothers," he said.

Jade and Jackie raced around the corner to find him.

33

"Oh, no!" Jackie gasped when he saw the shelves and shelves of GnomeKops. They all looked exactly alike! "How are we going to find the GnomeKop with the talisman?"

"I have an idea," Jade told Jackie. Then she pretended to be upset. "Help!" she shouted. "TurboTroll has captured the Gnome princess!"

"The evil one will pay!" GnomeKop cried, and he hopped off the shelf.

"Good job," Jackie told her. "Your trick worked."

"Thanks, Jackie." Jade grinned. "Now watch this!" She made a fast dive to grab the toy.

"Gnome power!" the toy cried out, then blasted a green ray at her.

"Hey!" Jade jumped out of the

way. "Stop that!" she cried.

Zzzaaappp! GnomeKop fired his belt blaster again. This time it hit a huge mountain of stuffed animals. Hundreds of soft toys fell on top of Jade, burying her.

"Jade!" Jackie cried. He raced to help her. He did not see GnomeKop scamper away.

"Gnome power!" the toy shouted again. He turned a corner and ran into the next aisle.

"No—*big* power!" a deep voice said.

GnomeKop had run straight onto Tohru's huge feet!

Finn and Ratso were there, too.

In one gigantic hand, Tohru held The Seeker—a magic wand that can find a talisman wherever it may be hidden. The Seeker had led him straight to GnomeKop.

Tohru reached down with his other hand, and snatched the toy. He clasped it in his fist, lifting it up, up, up to his eye level.

"Huh?" GnomeKop gasped, seeing the giant man face to face.

Quickly, Finn ripped off Gnome-Kop's belt blaster. Ratso tied the powerful toy's hands and feet.

A moment later, The Dark Hand enforcers were gone. And they took GnomeKop and the rat talisman with them!

Back at The Dark Hand lair, the enforcers dropped GnomeKop on Valmont's desk.

"Troll armies are ready!" the toy cried. "GnomeKop must be freed!"

Valmont stared at GnomeKop. "What on earth is that silly little toy saying?" he demanded.

Ratso stepped forward to explain. "Well, you see, TurboTroll is Gnome-Kop's enemy. The Emperor of the Troll Castle *hates* gnomes because gnomes have magic powers. So GnomeKop uses his power belt to blast them, and . . ."

Shendu's dragon statue was behind Valmont's desk. His eyes glowed red. "Never mind," Shendu said. "Get the talisman!"

Valmont grabbed the toy and popped open the battery chamber. He tried to yank out the talisman. But

GnomeKop struggled and fought back.

"GnomeKop escaped the bald-headed giant's fortress!" the toy said. "He will escape *you* as well!"

Valmont stopped. His eyes opened wide. "'The bald-headed giant?'" he repeated. "Could he possibly mean Captain Black?"

"It does not matter," Shendu said. "Give me the talisman!"

"Wait." Valmont stopped. An evil idea flickered through his brain. "If this gnome escaped from Section Thirteen, then perhaps he can lead us back there."

Shendu gasped. "Ah! And then we will find the other talismans!"

Valmont nodded. "But if we want to follow him, we must leave the

38

talisman inside him," he explained.

He turned to GnomeKop with a sneaky smile. "Mighty warrior," he said to the toy, "we have just learned that TurboTroll has taken over the bald-headed giant's fortress."

"I will have his head!" GnomeKop cried.

"Good," Valmont said. He untied GnomeKop's hands and feet and let him go.

"Now all you have to do is follow the gnome," Valmont whispered to his men. "Follow him back to Section Thirteen, and get the talismans. Then we will have all the power in the world!"

Chapter 6

"Boy, I don't think I want to see another teddy for a long time," Jade said. She and Jackie were searching the toy store for GnomeKop.

"I'm just glad you're okay," Jackie replied.

"So we've checked the whole mall," Jade said. "And no GnomeKop. He's probably gone by now."

"We can't be sure," Jackie said.

Jade looked around the toy store.

Shelves were knocked over and toys were scattered everywhere. "GnomeKop sure does a lot of damage for a little runt," she said.

Jackie smiled. "Didn't I tell you that within every weakness lies strength?"

Jade couldn't help thinking about all the damage *she* had caused. Jackie's broken leg. The talisman getting into GnomeKop.

I wish I would hurry up and find *my* strength already, she thought. Then she noticed something. "Jackie—look!" She pointed toward the end of the aisle.

GnomeKop marched back into the store. He stopped and sniffed the air.

"That toy is going *down!*" Jade cried.

"Shh!" Jackie pulled Jade onto his

41

lap and quickly wheeled behind a large Lego sculpture. He pointed to Tohru, Ratso, and Finn. They were following the toy.

"I bet GnomeKop is retracing his steps," Jackie said.

"But then The Dark Hand guys can follow him back to Section Thirteen!" Jade cried. "And the other talismans!"

Jackie whipped out his cell phone. "I'll warn Captain Black."

"But how are you going to explain it?" Jade asked. "Captain Black won't believe The Dark Hand teamed up with a magic gnome, right?"

"Do you have a better idea?" Jackie asked.

Jade nodded. "Remember that

TurboTroll I've been wanting?" she asked with a smile.

"I hope this works," Jackie said. He quickly bought Jade a TurboTroll.

"It's a snap!" Jade said as they followed GnomeKop outside. "I told you. GnomeKop can *never* pass up a battle with TurboTroll." She held up a purple doll with pink hair. "As soon as GnomeKop sees this guy, he'll go after him. We'll use TurboTroll to lead GnomeKop *away* from Section Thirteen."

Jade and Jackie hid around a corner. Jade held out the TurboTroll, so that GnomeKop could see it. "TurboTroll rules!" she cried.

GnomeKop stopped. He turned

43

and spotted Jade's toy. He rushed toward it. "Must destroy TurboTroll!" he shouted.

"It's working!" Jade whispered to Jackie. "Let's go!"

Jade and Jackie hurried down the street. They led GnomeKop toward the pier—far away from Section Thirteen.

Tohru, Finn, and Ratso followed GnomeKop.

"Are you sure this thing isn't lost?" Finn asked Tohru.

Tohru shrugged, and they kept following.

Every few blocks, Jackie and Jade stopped to hide behind a building.

"Come and get me Gnome-*wimp!*" Jade cried, holding out the troll again.

"Must destroy TurboTroll!" Gnome-

Kop repeated. "Destroy him!"

Finally they all reached the marina. Boats were docked all along the pier.

"Where should we go now?" Jade asked Jackie when they reached the end of a dock. Suddenly Jade's plan didn't seem so smart. She couldn't lead GnomeKop into the water. If she did, the talisman would be lost at the bottom of the bay!

Jackie didn't answer.

"Jackie?" she said. But Jackie wasn't there. Jade looked behind her.

Uh-oh. Jackie's wheelchair was stuck on a plank at the other end of the dock. He couldn't move. And The Dark Hand thugs were coming up right behind him!

"Watch out!" Jade cried, running to help.

But it was too late. Tohru was already tying Jackie into his wheelchair with some rope left lying on the dock.

Jackie gazed up at the huge man. "Uh, hi," Jackie said nervously. "Want to sign my cast?"

Tohru laughed and tied the rope tighter.

"Leave him alone!" Jade yelled at Tohru.

Finn and Ratso grabbed her.

Tohru lifted Jackie's wheelchair up, and over his head—with Jackie in it!

Then he tossed the whole thing into the bay!

"Jackieeeeee!" Jade cried.

Chapter 7

"Noooooooooo!" Jade yelled. She watched Jackie's wheelchair sink into the murky water. She wanted to jump in to save him, but Finn and Ratso were holding her tightly.

"Have a nice swim, Chan!" Finn called out.

"Yeah—hope you haven't eaten for an hour!" Ratso added with a laugh.

"Ratso!" Tohru boomed. "Get the gnome!"

Ratso let go of Jade and tried to grab GnomeKop.

But GnomeKop was still on the hunt for TurboTroll. Ratso could not catch him.

"Let go!" Jade cried. She twisted her body into a kung fu move and broke Finn's hold.

Then she grabbed TurboTroll from the dock and ran over to Tohru. "Hey—GnomeKop!" she called. "Are you looking for this?"

She waved the purple doll in the air. Then she shoved the TurboTroll up into Tohru's pant leg! That should keep the big guy busy, Jade thought.

"Gnome power!" GnomeKop cried. He raced to fight his enemy—inside Tohru's pants!

"Aaahhh!" Tohru cried as the battle between the two enemies began.

Jade turned to the water. "Hang on, Jackie! Here I come!" she cried, and she dove in after him.

Jade swam deeper and deeper. She searched for Jackie. But it was muddy down there. And cold. She couldn't find him anywhere.

Jade started to panic. I'm too late! He's gone—all the way to the bottom!

Finally, she couldn't hold her breath any longer. Her lungs felt as if they were going to burst.

Jade kicked hard, shooting up to the surface. She burst out of the water, gasping for air.

"Jade!" Jackie cried, splashing beside her.

49

"Jackie!" Jade opened her mouth too soon. Lots of water rushed in. She sputtered, coughing and spitting. But she was all right. And so was Jackie! "How . . .?" she asked him.

"I untied the ropes," Jackie explained. "Never mind. We've got to get GnomeKop before The Dark Hand does!"

Jackie pointed to Tohru. He was still hopping around and yelling on the dock.

Jade climbed out of the water, then helped Jackie out. He sat on the edge of the pier.

Tohru looked really angry. He reached into his pants and finally yanked out the GnomeKop. He squeezed the doll tightly.

"Unhand me, giant!" GnomeKop demanded. He chomped down on Tohru's hand.

Tohru hollered in pain. Then he tossed the GnomeKop away with incredible force!

The talisman burst out of the doll.

Jade watched the rat talisman soar through the air. Wow! Tohru is really powerful, she thought. When he throws something, he means it!

The flying talisman went farther . . . and farther . . . and farther. . . .

"Oops," Tohru said. He and the other enforcers ran after the talisman.

"Go, go, go!" Jackie cried to Jade. He quickly hobbled down the dock after them. "We can't let them get the talisman!"

Jade raced alongside Jackie. She stopped when she realized where the rat talisman was headed.

A fair was being held at the other end of the pier. A sign at the entrance to the event said: WELCOME TO GNOME DAY!

A giant GnomeKop stood underneath the sign. It was a huge balloon, more than fifty feet tall. It was right in the path of the flying talisman. And its mouth was wide open!

Jade gulped. "Uh-oh."

Chapter 8

"Hurry!" Jackie cried. He and Jade had reached the entrance to the GnomeKop fair—too late.

They watched the talisman sail right into the mouth of the gigantic GnomeKop balloon.

A moment later, the giant Gnome-Kop sprang to life!

Jade gasped. "No . . . way."

The giant GnomeKop marched forward. "Where is TurboTroll?" he

53

boomed. His voice was so loud, it hurt Jade's ears.

Jackie's eyes were open wide. So were Tohru's. Finn and Ratso stood there, shaking in fear. All of them were stunned by the enormous size of the giant GnomeKop.

"Where is TurboTroll?" the giant demanded again.

A smile crept across Jade's face. She had an awesome idea. "It's in his pants!" she shouted, pointing to Tohru.

"No!" Tohru cried. "No, no, nooooo!" He turned and stomped away as fast as he could.

"Run!" Ratso and Finn yelled, passing Tohru.

"TurboTroll!" the giant GnomeKop

cried. *Boom, boom, boom!* The ground shook as he followed them.

Jade watched, totally stunned.

Jackie cleared his throat. "Jade, we must go after the talisman," he reminded her.

Jade stared at him. "You're kidding, right?

". . . so while Jackie kept the giant GnomeKop busy, I climbed up top, crawled inside his mouth, and got the talisman!" Jade explained to Uncle later that day. She and Jackie were safely back home.

"You did very well, Jade!" Uncle said.

Jade gave Uncle a weak smile. "Yeah. Except for the part where I slipped and fell off the GnomeKop . . . and landed on Jackie."

"And broke my other leg!" Jackie groaned, touching his new cast. "It's hard to believe. I escape an exploding bridge, fly through the air, get thrown into the ocean . . . and nothing happens. Still, I have *two* broken legs. One from a toy—and one from my niece!"

"Sorry!" Jade said for the hundredth time. "At least the rat talisman is safe in the Section Thirteen vault, right?"

Jackie smiled. "That is true," he said. "And you also found your greatest strength, Jade."

"I did?" Jade asked.

Jackie nodded. "You did not give up, no matter how badly things went.

Not many people have that quality."

Jade beamed. "I'm no quitter!" She glanced at Jackie's cast. "So maybe I should try to take care of you again—until you're back on your feet."

"No!" Jackie said. "Uh, I mean . . . maybe you could help me find a talisman—when I'm better."

"Yippee!" Jade cried. "How long does it take to fix a broken leg?"

Uncle started to laugh. "Don't worry," he told her. "Remember, Jackie is young and strong. He will heal quickly."

"Right," Jade said. "And when Jackie is ready to look for another talisman, I'll be ready to help him!"

A letter to you from Jackie

Dear Friends,

In _The Power of the Rat_, Jade blames herself when I trip over her GnomeKop and break my leg. She also feels awful when she lets the rat talisman fall into GnomeKop's battery chamber. Then I tell her a secret I learned a long time ago: within every weakness lies strength.

I still try to remind myself of this every day. You see, I have a weakness that not many people know about.

When I was young, my parents were very poor. They had to move to Australia to make money. They sent me to a school called the Chinese Opera Research Institute. The focus of the school was on acting and martial arts—not math, science, and reading.

I knew that life would be hard if I did not master these subjects. But I had to make the best of what I was offered. I had to learn as much as possible about acting, martial arts, and most importantly, discipline. All of my hard work paid off, and I developed a successful career in film and television!

Don't let my success fool you, though. It was really hard getting where I am today. I had to work twice as much the others because I didn't have the basic educational skills they had.

Education is still very important to me. That's why I started an organization that gives scholarships to kids. I want them to have an easier time reaching their goals than I did. In a way, I'm using my weakness to give strength to others!

Even Jade finds her strength through her faults. If she did not make so many mistakes, she would never know how determined she is.

So remember, nobody is perfect. But it's what you learn from your weakness that builds great strength.

Jackie Chan

Find out what happens in the next book!

#9 Stronger Than Stone

The Dark Hand gives Jackie a potion that will turn him into stone. There's only one way Jade can get the cure—to give The Dark Hand all the talismans. What will she do?

JACKIE CHAN ADVENTURES™ #9

As seen on Kids' WB!

"Your mind is your greatest strength!"

Inside: A cool trading card and a letter from Jackie!

Stronger Than Stone

JACKIE CHAN ADVENTURES